Dreams

Dreams

EZRA JACK KEATS

PUFFIN BOOKS

For Mitsue Ishitake,
Sachiko Saionji,
Yosuke Seki,
and my friends
of the Ohanashi Caravan

It was hot.
After supper Roberto came
to his window to talk with Amy.
"Look what I made in school today—
a paper mouse!"
"Does it do anything?" Amy asked.
Roberto thought for a while.
"I don't know," he said. Then he put
the mouse on the windowsill.

As it grew darker, the city got quieter.
"Bedtime, Roberto," called his mother.
"Bedtime for you, too,"
 other mothers called.
"Good-night, Amy."
"Good-night, Roberto."
"G-o-o-o-o-d-night!" echoed the parrot.
Soon they were all in bed.

Someone began to dream.

Soon everybody was dreaming—
except one person.

Somehow Roberto just couldn't fall asleep.
It got later and later.

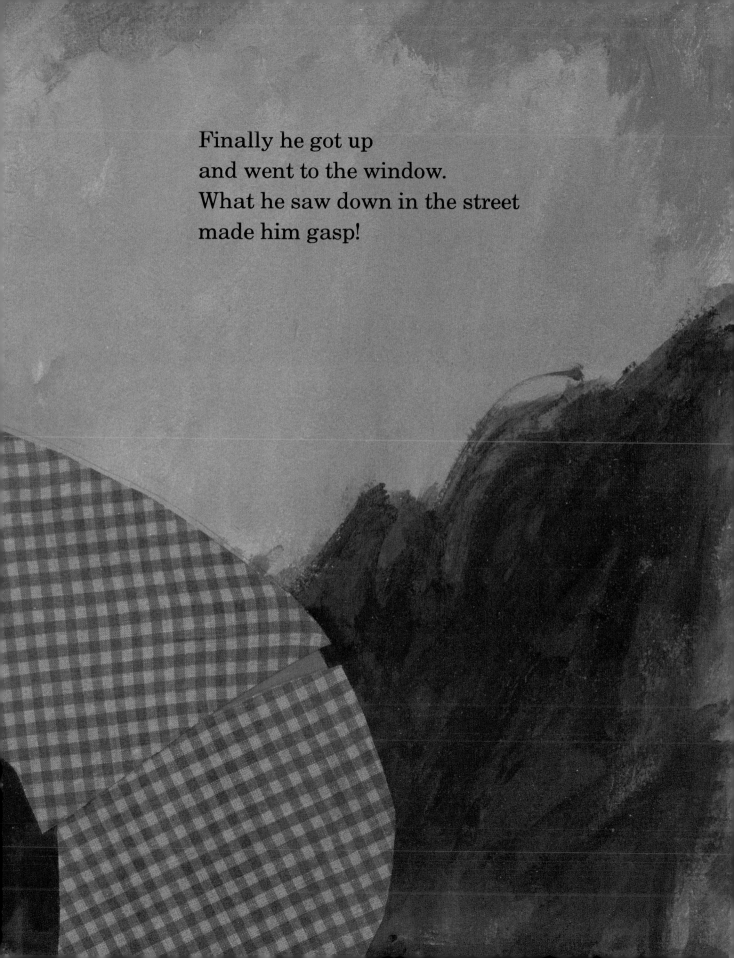

Finally he got up
and went to the window.
What he saw down in the street
made him gasp!

There was Archie's cat!
A big dog had chased him into a box.
The dog snarled.
"He's trapped!" thought Roberto.
"What should I do?"

Then it happened!
His pajama sleeve
brushed the paper mouse
off the windowsill.
It sailed away from him.

Down it fell,
turning this way
and that,
casting a big shadow
on the wall.

The shadow grew bigger—
and bigger—

and BIGGER!
The dog howled and ran away.

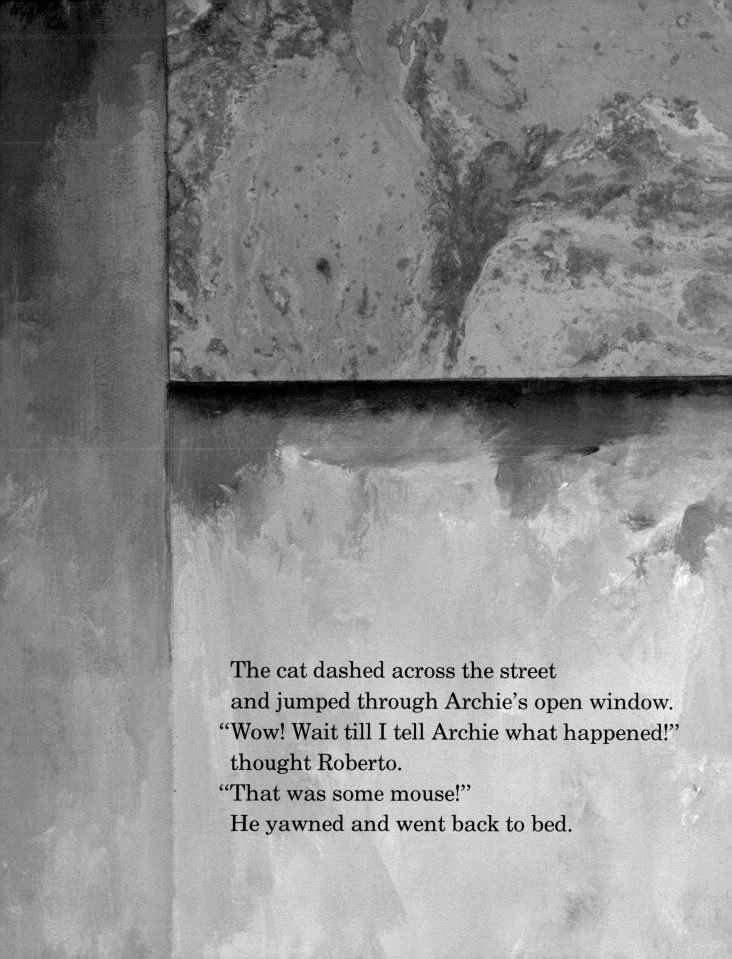

The cat dashed across the street
and jumped through Archie's open window.
"Wow! Wait till I tell Archie what happened!"
thought Roberto.
"That was some mouse!"
He yawned and went back to bed.

Morning came, and everybody
was getting up.
Except one person.

Roberto was fast asleep, dreaming.

PUFFIN BOOKS
Published by the Penguin Group
Penguin Putnam Books for Young Readers, 345 Hudson Street, New York, New York 10014, U.S.A.
Penguin Books Ltd, 27 Wrights Lane, London W8 5TZ, England
Penguin Books Australia Ltd, Ringwood, Victoria, Australia
Penguin Books Canada Ltd, 10 Alcorn Avenue, Toronto, Ontario, Canada M4V 3B2
Penguin Books (N.Z.) Ltd, 182-190 Wairau Road, Auckland 10, New Zealand

Penguin Books Ltd, Registered Offices: Harmondsworth, Middlesex, England

First published in the United States of America by Macmillan Publishing Co., Inc., 1974
Published by Viking and Puffin Books, divisions of Penguin Putnam Books for Young Readers, 2000

30

LIBRARY OF CONGRESS CATALOGING-IN-PUBLICATION DATA

Keats, Ezra Jack.
Dreams / Ezra Jack Keats.
p.   cm.
Summary: One night while everyone is sleeping, a little boy
watches his paper mouse save a cat from an angry dog.
ISBN 978-0-670-89225-9 (hardcover) — ISBN 978-0-14-056744-1 (pbk.)
[1. Night—Fiction. 2. Paper work—Fiction. 3. Hispanic
Americans—Fiction.] I. Title.
PZ7.K2253 Dr 2000 [E]—dc21 00-008643

Manufactured in China